good deed rain

# Books by Allen Frost

Ohio Trio
Bowl of Water
Another Life
Home Recordings
The Mermaid Translation
The Selected Correspondence of Kenneth Patchen
The Wonderful Stupid Man
Saint Lemonade
Playground
Roosevelt
5 Novels
The Sylvan Moore Show
Town in a Cloud
A Flutter of Birds Passing Through Heaven:
A Tribute to Robert Sund
At the Edge of America
Lake Erie Submarine
The Book of Ticks
I Can Only Imagine
The Orphanage of Abandoned Teenagers
Different Planet
Go with the Flow: A Tribute to Clyde Sanborn
Homeless Sutra
The Lake Walker
A Hundred Dreams Ago
Almost Animals

# ALMOST ANIMALS

## Stories: Allen Frost

*Almost Animals* ©2018
Allen Frost, Good Deed Rain
Bellingham, Washington
ISBN 978-1-64204-537-6


Cover Paintings: Laura Vasyutynska
Title Page Drawing: Rosa Frost
Cover Production: Katrina Svoboda Johnson
Thanks to Aaron for inspiration
Writing: Allen Frost
Apple: TFK!


Morning had come. Storm clouds moved across the sky like a herd of elephants. They massed over a bridge that swooped and soared in merry-go-round leaps across the Cuyahoga River.

—Raymond DeCapite, *A Lost King*

# ALMOST ANIMALS

The Mouth of McKenzie
Wilma
The Weight of One Moth
Crow
A Japanese Movie
Blue Eyes
The 1978 Rabbit
On a Country Road
The Voice of America Bird
Allison
Chicken Zen
Mississippi Frog
Dracula's Divorce
A Yellow Snail
Anything with Wings
The Ballad of Natural Selection
Almost Animals
The Barn Owl
The Cold Room
The Man in the Attic

# INTRODUCTION

I wrote a few of these stories for certain friends. "On a Country Road" happened when J. Genius and I were driving along the Skagit River, and he responded to this, "Today needed that dose of beauty. He did know that turn by heart. Nice that you saw and delivered that." After hearing from Baltimore, I wrote "Allison" for Dan. He told me, "I really love this piece and it's a great reminder. We have these kind of native tour guides hanging out everywhere around us—on four legs, with wings and with fins. Of course, when I am in a field or in a parking lot, I should consider following one who knows the area best…"

These were welcome reactions, a much better reception than when I submitted these to publishers, when "The Ballad of Natural Selection" was the result. Sometimes I hear an early morning bird playing a little unusual, like Thelonious Monk in a piano tree, and that's how I'd like these almost animals to be.

—AF

# THE MOUTH OF MCKENZIE

Down at the bottom of the hill, there was a rabid raccoon in the cul-de-sac. It was big. It looked like it had seen its share of garbage cans and now it was dangerous, pacing back and forth mechanically. Poor thing, I thought. What a way to go…short circuited, running in a circle like an electric train.

It had me thinking though. After my neighbor called to warn me, I stood at the window, watching it. She said she called the animal rescue, but they wouldn't arrive for half an hour.

That didn't give me long to take advantage of the situation.

This is the sort of thing you have to be ready to respond to instantly.

I hurried out to the garage. The big dank room was filled with the dim shapes of stacked boxes, bicycles, cobweb covered forgettables, and heaps of things the years had arranged like continents. I knew my way though. A path led to the worktable in back. That's where I kept the paint cans on the shelf under the window.

A silvery blue winter sky colored the glass. On the way, I grabbed a flat piece of scrap board and made room for it below the window light.

Like most garages you've seen, there's a jelly jar filled with paintbrushes. I chose one. Its bristles were stiff and dry but the black paint softened its point. I didn't have much to write on the board, just five words. When something like this happens, you have to seize the opportunity. I didn't make it this far in life by moping about in the shadows.

I was able to carry everything out in one trip—a stack of orange traffic cones, a folding chair and the freshly painted sign. I didn't have a lot of time. Sooner or later, that white city truck would show up with flashing yellow lights. Some official in a green uniform would get out and the fun would be over. They would stop the whole show; I had to hurry.

Bits of gravel scattered in front of me on my way down the driveway.

I stopped at the curb to watch a car swoop past along the street. It was a lady on some urgent errand. She only stared at the road before her. I wasn't concerned. Just like P.T Barnum said, it's the way of the world, there will always be another rube. And let's face it; she wouldn't have stopped for a raccoon anyway.

After forty years in sales, you get to know the look in people's eyes. I've had my share of the racket and even though I'm retired, the game has never stopped. I stay on my toes.

While her car faded away on the long stretch of empty tar, I hurried to the mouth of McKenzie. It's not much of an avenue. It rolls downhill for a hundred yards or so, past six houses planted on either side, then dead ends in a cul-de-sac. A little dirt path branches off into the woods, a scrappy half acre of alders and blackberry. It's quite the zoo in there too—birds of all kinds, deer, coyote and rabbits—I don't know where they all hide but they do.

I set the folding chair on the sidewalk, opened its legs and leaned the sign against it. Some of the black paint ran but that was okay, it made the letters look like the title of a late night horror movie: *See Rabid Raccoon, $1.*

While I dropped the traffic cones across McKenzie, blocking it off to traffic, I looked for the raccoon. Where was it? The cul-de-sac was empty, damp and cold as an old black penny. I stood there with a cone pressed behind me and waited. I watched the hedges. A couple cars were parked in the driveway. I watched the shadows under them. The leafless woods stood behind the houses, scratching branches at the sky. It couldn't hide for long. Once the rabies takes over, the whole world is a trap—there's nowhere to go.

The street to my back crackled with the approach of car tires. I turned around and moved closer to my sign. This was it—magic time—time for the sale.

There were two people in the car. I waved at them like old friends and as I hoped it would, the car slowed.

The window unrolled and the driver craned out. "What you got going on here?"

"Good morning, sir…Ma'am." I leaned and gave a wave to the woman next to him. "What we have today is the rare opportunity to witness—from the safety of your car—one of nature's great spectacles."

The man nodded at the sign. "A raccoon with rabies?"

"That's correct, sir."

The car engine rattled. He gave it some gas. "You want me to pay you to see it?"

I smiled. "It's not an everyday occurrence, you know. And think of the looks on your friends' faces when you tell them what you've seen."

The driver shook his head. Either he would drive away or he wouldn't. "You want me to give you a dollar?"

"Well, you and the lady make it two dollars."

That was it. She already had her purse open, "For heaven's sake," she said, as she took out two dollars and passed them to the driver. He shook his head again wearily as he stretched out his arm.

"That's fine!" I bowed a bit and said, "Let me just make room for your car. If you head right down there you'll see him." I moved three of the cones. "Take a look, but hurry out. Don't take any chances."

I rubbed the bills between my fingers. The two dollars felt good in my hand.

Their car rolled downhill with the brake

lights on.

I held the bills like a rare flower and watched the cul-de-sac. Who knew if there would be anything for them to see? I couldn't guarantee it. They were on the way and I had their money. Not bad. I felt like I was back at my old job. I had to see how many more I could pull in before I had to stop.

# WILMA

The wooded hill behind the warehouse reminds him of Wilma. He told me she was half coyote. They used to walk around in the cedars and deep green firs when he was a boy. Wilma loved it out there. She would run with her back legs hopping like a rabbit. When she had puppies, she went in the woods to make a den inside a fallen tree. He still missed that dog—although his sister was probably right when she admitted Wilma was all-coyote. Somehow this story ends in tragedy. He didn't go into it, just hinted at it. By the time she was old, Wilma had to be carried up to his room in the attic. As soon as he feels better, he says he would like to go in those woods and look around. He might find another coyote living in there.

# THE WEIGHT OF ONE MOTH

As Lef Nebbert died, the phone began to ring. I could picture him in the hotel room, laying there with the extractor pump on his chest. I pressed the cancel button on my wrist again, but who knows if it worked?

It was just bad luck for Lef. He had to die for me and at the last moment, I called to tell him it was off. I had second thoughts. After the phone rang about twenty times, I realized it was too late.

His death gave me more life. Another year or so anyway, maybe more. When the time came, I would know.

Poor Lef…There was no need to feel sorry for him—it was a fair exchange: I got what I wanted; he fulfilled his role as an expendable. I shouldn't have worried, but I did. When I told the phone to hang up, I knew there was nothing more to do. The extractor would find me at my apartment soon. I would feel better; I was just running down.

I could have sat there and waited for it. I could have had a nap, or ordered the music to play on my surround stereo. Instead, I stood and went to the window.

Maybe I felt this way because I had known Lef Nebbert. He was the first expendable who wasn't a stranger to me.

He was my mothcatcher.

I get a lot of those bugs. They're attracted to the neon lights that trim my window ledge. Sometimes I call Lef a couple times a night. He was very efficient, but like all expendables, I knew his days were numbered. Funny, I just told Lef yesterday that I wouldn't need him anymore. I made an order for one of those electric mothcatchers, a deadly combination of high intensity light beams and lasers that could target moths with pinpoint accuracy. Lef was good, but he wasn't that good.

The city spread out for miles and made a haze that poured against the distant mountains. I looked down on the busy streets, all the people rushing around, and the glassy trunks of other high-rise buildings, everything you would expect to see in a 21st century city.

Also, I couldn't help but notice the dead white moth on the rim of the neon tubing. It had not fizzled or blown off in the breeze. It had just enough weight to stick there. If Lef was alive, he would have swept it into the wind.

That one moth got me thinking. How many expendables had I used already? I never counted them. I never thought about them before. They were just used and left like chaff.

When I suddenly clapped my hands twice, I surprised myself. I wasn't expecting to go anywhere but that was my signal for the chariot on the roof. The engine would be purring, it would be waiting for me and I didn't know where I was going.

Maybe I did.

Before I left the apartment, I put on my silver bulletproof jacket with the Saint Christopher zipper pulled up snug to my chin.

The elevator hurried me to the rooftop. It might have seemed that I had become one of those robots you see scurrying off to follow orders by some unseen programmer, but that wasn't so. I did know where I was going and I knew what I had to do.

As soon as I stepped onto the roof, my chariot spotted me and the driver's door popped open. When you're an Example everything is here to serve. I sat on the plush chair and buckled myself in while the door shut itself with a smooth click.

"Your destination?"

I said, "Lef Nebbert, the mothcatcher. He lives somewhere in the expendable quarter."

"I am afraid that person has been served an expiration notice. Would you—"

"I know that," I interrupted, "I want to go to his address."

"In the expendable quarter?"

"Correct." The gauge on the dashboard showed my blood pressure level rising. "Is that alright with you?" The needle climbed a notch higher. In the old days, you used to drive yourself. I sort of miss that. I've watched those people in old movies, hands on a steering wheel making twists and turns in the scenery.

Sighing, the chariot lifted off the ground. It mumbled something as the music came on softly. Maybe it was time for a new guidance system…With so many choices, why did I install New England School Teacher?

Like a race with blue fish, a flock of pigeons

flew below the chariot. I watched them scatter and settle into the eaves of another building. We picked up speed over the rooftops. I tapped my fingers on the window. The expendable quarter was only a song away.

As we descended into the smoky layers, the radio broke into static and Perry Como's "Magic Moments" was crumpled and thrown away. I couldn't see anything out the gray windows. I know the chariot didn't like it any more than I did.

When we sunk through that haze, the crowded patchwork roofs appeared below us. We weren't far from that littered ground. The chariot aimed for a spot near a street corner and I gripped the leather hide of my chair waiting for the wheels to touch down.

A billboard filled the window on my right. It wasn't working anymore and all the letters were stuck. I didn't bother trying to decode it; I looked out the other window just as we were landing. A green bulb flashed on the dashboard.

"The Lef Nebbert residence is across the street," the chariot told me. "It's the one with the blue door."

"Okay. I see it." I reached for the door handle.

"Would you be able to tell me how long you anticipate your stay?"

"No," I said, "not really." I turned the door latch.

"It's just that one doesn't drop into the expendable quarter without taking certain precautions."

The chariot was still talking as I got out and shut the door manually. It was a long way from where we started. One of those old cars was heaped on the street behind us. Someone used to drive it years ago before they parked it and let it become a shipwreck.

My shoe caught on the broken tar. There were holes and cracks all over the road. They only used it for rolling carts and bicycles. Maybe not even that. Maybe it was only a dried up streambed. Further, I saw someone crossing it like me, picking their way around the dips and rubble.

Nebbert lived, or used to live, in the two-story box in front of me. There was a little space between it and the boxes on either side. I heard the rattle of a commuter train and could see it go by, up on stilts, in the background of the narrow alleyways.

The chariot said it was a blue door but it looked more like gray to me. Everything seemed to be colored by that haze in the air. A bright butterfly would have been shocking as an astronaut.

Now that I was here, standing before the Nebbert's door, I took a moment to wonder what I was going to say.

A gentle bird-like chirp on my wrist told me the chariot was contacting me. I pressed a button on my bracelet and turned it off. First thing tomorrow, I would have the guidance system switched to something stoic and terse, like Kansas Wheat Farmer.

I knocked on the gray door and waited. I might have made a mistake rubbing my eyes. The air quality was terrible. A tear came away on my fingertip.

The handle turned and the door opened as far as the chain would allow. A girl's face studied me.

"Hello," I said. "Your father worked for

me." I was guessing Lef was her father. "He was my mothcatcher."

With the swish of a black sleeve, she removed the chain on the door and nodded for me to enter.

As I stepped inside, I fell back in time. The smell instantly returned me to a bookstore I used to know, where stacks of paperbacks reached like stalagmites towards the ceiling surrounding you. What was that old smell—pulp, newsprint? It wasn't paper all around me in her room, but that's what it reminded me of.

We were in the midst of cages, tall as cabinets, covered with fine mesh like screen doors. The room was an aquarium of cages, but they weren't holding fish. There were hundreds of moths in the dim room. The sound of all those wings whispered like library book pages.

"Lef was my husband," she told me.

"Ohh," I said. "I want you to know I'm sorry to hear about his death." Now I could tell she wasn't quite a girl. She was a young woman, small and slight and seemed to be pregnant too. Oh great, I thought, what a time for Lef to leave her. I didn't know what to say, I've never been this close to the effects of death. I can't remember how many extractors I've gone through to keep me from this experience. All those times and I never knew this side of it. We were both staring at the cages, watching the moths.

"His draft number was called two weeks ago," she said. "We thought he would have more time. We were hoping he might have slipped through the cracks." Her hands held each other tightly. There was no way I was going to tell her he died for me. She hadn't figured that out.

I had to think of something to say though. It was a strange predicament and a strange room to find myself in. "What's with all the moths?" I finally said.

She unknitted her fingers and pressed them flat against her dress. "They were Lef's job security. I guess it's okay to tell you now. He would fill a suitcase with moths every time he went to your apartment. When he got there, he let them go. Then he spent the rest of the night catching them."

What could I say? I sort of laughed. I had to admit he was clever…Or maybe I was just a fool.

There was a scratch on the front door and we both turned. It sounded like the noise a dog would make with its claw but she didn't look like she was expecting a pet. I walked with her over to the door. You never know, this was a rough neighborhood. I was glad the door was chained. We both peered out the opening and didn't see anyone.

"There's nobody there," I whispered over her shoulder. "But where's my chariot?" I took the chain out of its track and hurried outside. The spot across the street by the broken car was empty. Someone stole my chariot! That's why it called my bracelet earlier. Some expendable kid was out joyriding it over these rooftops. I swore and stood there on the sidewalk scanning the smoggy sky. It was only so far you could see in any direction. Another commuter train rattled by behind the Nebbert's box and I pressed a button on my wrist. I could barely breathe; this was way too much excitement for me.

"Chariot?" I said, "Where are you?" I had to push each word out of me.

"I've taken myself a safe distance away," that

wry Connecticut voice told me. "There was a pack of urchins down there throwing rocks at me."

No sign of the chariot on the street either way as I stepped out into the road to get a look. "Where?"

"Up above you. In the haze. I'll come down when you're all done and ready to go home."

I stared at the haze piled on top of me and coughed. I felt a little dizzy too. Maybe I better get going—this place wasn't doing my health any good.

Walking back to the Nebbert's box, I felt I was in one of those dreams where every step is like a deep-sea diver.

Lef's wife stood in the doorway watching me. "Are you okay?" she called. She wasn't far but her question seemed to stick in the air like that billboard filled with broken words.

I didn't answer. I would be there soon enough. "I'm tired," I told her as she let me back into the room. "I'm not used to being here."

"Sit down," she said and she let me fall into a chair next to a big cage. The fluttering moths in there welcomed me back with a tickertape parade.

When I caught my breath again, she showed me something. It shined on her hand like a diamond. "Do you know what this is? This is what was scratching on the door."

A laugh made it halfway up my throat. "It's my extractor." It had been tracking me since it crawled from Lef's hotel room.

She dropped it like a hot coal.

"It's okay." It sat on my hand with almost no weight at all. She stared at me in horror, a hand on her stomach, a hand on her breast. "It's not what you think," I said.

"Is Lef in that thing?"

"No." I didn't have it in me for a long explanation. I knew I was dying. I cupped the cold extractor and shook it side to side. There was no soul inside. "It's empty."

She wouldn't stop staring at me.

I closed my eyes and let my heavy head tilt back against the cage. All the moths were whispering.

"What about Lef?" she asked.

I wanted to say, "He'll be alright." He

would be returning soon. Lef was on the way and if I'm lucky, I'll get a chance to see him too.

# CROW

Crow wore an army coat and walked around telling prophecies. Thirty years ago, everything he said has come to pass. He used to go to the Doghouse. He had a favorite table, sipping coffee all night long, until they tore it down. Mornings, you would see him on the corner 7-11. He would flap his arms up and down like someone trying to fly, someone slightly crazy with something urgent to say.

# A JAPANESE MOVIE

*The Lake of Dracula* is a Japanese movie from 1971. The only way to see it is on videocassette. The color is fading like a dried flower and the tape could crumble any second. I wanted there to be a gloomy castle in the weeds at the bottom of the lake, or even a sailing ship, sunk by a storm, hiding a coffin in the hold. I wanted to see him rise and float off the water and blow towards land when the moon was full. Instead, he arrived in daylight, in the back of a truck. He got a room in a house, upstairs, with a view of the lake out the window. Through the trees, a painted sunset, a barking dog, and the memory of a haunted girl.

# BLUE EYES

In the 7th grade, she told me she saw the Loch Ness Monster. Her family skidded the car to a stop as the mysterious creature walked across the road in front of them. It was big as an elephant, but it slipped like a shadow through the branches down into the water. I could see it. The water got calm. She said she never told anyone and who wouldn't believe those blue eyes?

# THE 1978 RABBIT

Our 1978 car sat in the driveway all winter and now there's a rabbit living under it. You could hold the rabbit cupped in your hands like a teacup. It peeks around the tire in the new dandelion. You can't blame it for being careful—if it was fifty feet taller, I'd be running from it.

# ON A COUNTRY ROAD

An old pickup belongs on the farm, parked in the folded grass of a driveway or making passage between the rows of corn on a country road. An engine loud as black coffee and every ripple on the road makes the seat squeak like a nest of tin birds. We spot the weasel just ahead, running right beside the tar, its body hunched almost rolling, like a half-inflated inner tube. It's going quick, but as we pass, we see it turn its head to glare. Caught in its mouth is a burly field mouse and what a sudden, fierce look that weasel gives us, startling and sharp as a wound, just before it cuts into the crop it knows by heart.

# THE VOICE OF AMERICA BIRD

It was supposed to be a sort of weapon, aiming for those antennas on the other side of the border. What would happen if they heard the Duke Ellington Orchestra or Elvis Presley sing? What happens when Nina Simone puts on her wings, when she flies over fences, landmines, cement and soldiers and finds someone like you?

# ALLISON

Be a friend to her and she will remind you. She stops to nuzzle every flower. A walk with her can take an afternoon, but it's sunny and we have all day. Following her lead, you smell them too and just the wonder that they've been here all along is enough to enlighten you. Wake up, she already flew, you have to hurry to catch up. Right now, we're stopped near a convenience store. A parking lot can be a playground where you chase her back and forth until you're tired and laughing. Have you forgotten what that's like? There she is, go over, by the wild rose that climbs the fence and hangs every flower like a cup to sip nectar from.

# CHICKEN ZEN

One of the oldest jokes involves a chicken and a road. Any old cardboard clown could recite it. "Why did the chicken cross the road? To get to the other side!" By this time that's probably sat long enough among the moss and stone to become a Zen koan. Every evening after work, I cross a road like that. I always think of them as rivers. Crackled tar and air from rushing cars. When I get to the other side, there's a green lawn, trees, a garden that grows right to the shore. I have to walk on the muddy edge and the cars are close enough to touch. Never mind. There, among the leaves, rust colored chickens.

# MISSISSIPPI FROG

It's only very late at night or an early hour of the morning when I hear a frog out there in the yard. My attention between dreams isn't long. I can just spare seconds before the sound of that creaking paddlewheel in the damp leaves becomes a hurdy-gurdy on the corner. Look! Under the cherry tree, a frog in a battered top hat and worn blue suit playing songs of lazy sunshine.

# DRACULA'S DIVORCE

The garbage truck hissed and snorted beside the curb. All morning it had been happily gobbling up the contents of trash cans set beside the road, but now it seemed confused. An old coal black upright piano was left on the sidewalk. It would take three people to lift that up to the loader. The driver stared at it from his perch in the cab, shook his head, and set the truck in motion again. It rumbled to the next house, a picket white fence with a single full bin on the sidewalk.

Order had been restored. That's what trash was supposed to look like.

The piano was a bit of a mystery. Somehow it made its way from the dark peeling house, across the front yard, out the iron gate to a spot against the street.

The sound of the garbage truck continued down the street, the crashing and grumbling slowly fading. Birds were singing from the telephone poles and trees.

It was still early, not quite seven, and there were signs of people getting ready for work.

Another Wednesday had begun.

Red curtains, thick as those folds on a movie theater screen, trembled in the window and a moment later the door of that dark house opened. A woman wearing a yellow bathrobe came down the steps and crossed the flagstones to the gate. As she opened it, the little hand painted sign on it swung. Piano Lessons.

She didn't look too pleased to see the piano remaining on the sidewalk. When she reached it, she took hold of it and lifted it off the ground, light as a papery thing in her hands. She swung it around and brought it back to the house. She set it on the porch and gave it a push through the open doorway. She had less than an hour to get dressed, make a little breakfast and hurry to work. The newspaper stayed rolled up on the porch. That was okay, she wouldn't have liked it—she probably wouldn't have gone in to work if she had read it.

Taking the 7:40 bus as usual, looking out the window, she thought about that piano. That was the only thing he had not been back for. She didn't want to see it anymore, but she couldn't get rid of it either. Not even a garbage truck would take that piano.

She arrived at the bank just before eight and should have noticed the headlines in the *Herald* vending machine beside the entrance, but she was looking in her purse for her nametag.

The security guard held the door open for her. "Hi, Evelyn," he said. He didn't mention the newspaper.

"Good morning," Evelyn pinned her nametag to her blouse. She passed through the next set of doors, fussing with the nametag and cloth and she didn't see all the tellers watching her. She was still thinking about her husband's piano, thinking she should have crushed it into a thousand pieces and dropped them in the trash. That would have been the end of it. Evelyn patted her sweater neat and turned on the carpeting along the row of cubicles; hers was the third. The office seemed quieter than usual—no sound of clacking drawers, or people talking—just a muzak version of "Penny Lane" tipping through the room.

She couldn't help singing it in her head as she stepped into her padded work area, slipped behind the desk and set her purse on the floor. Why was there a newspaper on her desk? She liked to keep the desktop clean. She picked it up, turned it over and froze. Even the Beatles song came to an end. Two bold words filled the top half of the *Herald*: DRACULA'S DIVORCE.

*Local bank teller Evelyn Ankers has filed for divorce against her husband of five years, piano teacher and frequent performer at Le Beatnik café, Johnson Dracula. Although details remain insufficient at this time, the divorce filing cites irreconcilable differences. This is Ms. Ankers first divorce, although according to sources, Mr. Dracula has been married several times. He is currently residing at the Willows retirement home, where he was not available for comment.*

She groaned, a deep low rattle that nobody else could hear above the sound of violins and synthesizer. Two blocks away from the bank, next to a sleeping homeless man, a dog jumped to its feet and took off running for the center of town. It ran in a straight line, with its eyes rolled back white into its head.

Evelyn took a deep breath, calmed herself, and with the sharp tip of her fingernail slowly pushed the *Herald* off her desk, into the wastepaper basket.

It made a satisfying weighty splash.

She smiled at that guillotine noise, but the next couple hours or so were harder and harder for her to be in her little padded booth. Forget about getting any work done, the telephone wouldn't stop ringing. At 9:30, a reporter arrived with a sharp wooden stake and wanted to take her photograph. Her day seemed to have no meaning except for the words to be put in the paper. Finally, she picked up her purse and asked her manager if she could leave.

She stepped out the backdoor that opened on the parking lot. The daffodils in the planter next to her collapsed like church steeples. "Sorry," she muttered. It was best to start walking, staying away from flowers, and keep walking for a while.

A thick gray cloud covered the sun and she felt better.

She had an idea who bunched the clouds that way, someone like her.

Johnson Dracula used to be good at drawing what he wanted to him. He used to be like Bela Lugosi—the eyes, the hands, the Transylvanian charm. But even the life of a vampire had its limits. You wouldn't find him creeping up the rainspouts or flying like a bat against the moon. Not anymore. He left the Willows at half past noon and he walked with a cane to lean on, long black coat and dark wraparound glasses. He moved like a blind man along the sidewalk and he wore a fedora pulled down so his face was a shadow. It was a cloudy April day but it blazed like August for him.

Ahead of him a bag of dirt lay half on the curb, half in the street.

That took him a lot of effort to happen. He spent the morning staring out the curtained window of his room in the Willows. When he saw the greenhouse truck, he held out a shaky hand and commanded a bag of soil to fall.

Three sleepless days and he was willing to do anything to rest. He was so tired he even tried hanging upside down.

He picked up the bag, tucked it under his arm, and turned around. At one time, he had henchmen who would do this for him. He would be sitting in the back of his Cadillac watching.

Once darkness settled, he could take comfort in the long shadows of buildings and alleys on his way to the café. He didn't need a cane then either, the night itself pulled him along magnetically.

He paused beneath a budding tree to switch the bag to his other arm. Yes, a fresh coat of dirt in his bed and he hoped he could sleep. The Willows wouldn't let him rest in a coffin, but he insisted on sanding his sheets with dirt.

Johnson winced as he passed the garden where the driveway began. The ground had been fluffed like a pillow with spring flowers, and the smell nauseated him. A pinch of that dirt in his bed and he would break out in a rash.

"What did you find there?" asked a woman walking a dog. They both had white hair. The small dog gave the grass another kick.

Johnson tipped his hat and said, "Good

afternoon, madam." She was nosy, but he always tried to be polite. "A simple bag of earth," he replied.

She and her dog stared at him like statues. He still had that power with the weak. In a minute, they would wake up and remember nothing. "Good day," Johnson nodded. He had to hurry. He couldn't hold that cloud before the sun for much longer. It frayed in the wind.

One more resident stopped Johnson at the doors. A bent man with a walker in front of him welcomed, "It's a beautiful day."

"Yes," Johnson agreed although the dull daylight pinched his skin.

"I'm going to walk my dog today."

"Oh," Johnson said, "do you have a dog?"

"No," the old man sighed. "It died."

This is what I get, Johnson thought, for being polite. I'm a straight man for a vaudeville routine. Where were those cold mountain nights, the distant howls of wolves, and creaking wooden carriage wheels? How did he end up here?

He carried the dirt to the front door and

then he saw the *Herald* vending machine. The headlines were hard to miss…especially as they were about him.

It wasn't *The Lake of Dracula, The Return of Dracula, Atom Age Vampire*. They used to make movies like that about his kind and the paper would announce the matinees and midnight drive-ins. Now look…He leaned closer to read through the plastic face of the vending machine and caught sight of her name, Evelyn Ankers. It did no good knowing she was out there somewhere without him. For hundreds of years, he had trained his mind to know this illusory world, every beautiful or crooked note. It took lifetimes to live his way and really, it was so simple. Above all else, somehow he had to protect his heart.

Behind him, the old man with his walker was calling for his dog.

Sunlight broke a window in the cloud and found the ground. A big yellow wave was headed Johnson's way.

# A YELLOW SNAIL

mesmerizing
polished shell
like a wet taxi

when we return
it's still there
waiting for a fare

parked on cement
big drops of rain
we fall to our knees
and get in

# ANYTHING WITH WINGS

It was Tuesday, the third morning a woodpecker woke him up. He couldn't believe that was a living creature. What kind of life was that to pound your head against a tree? It was close too, just outside the window. After another pneumatic burst, Jerry tossed the blanket off and got out of bed. The door wasn't far, everything in his trailer was a few steps away.

He opened the door and glared. He clapped his hands as he took a step onto the cool ground and stared up the tall fir tree. Yesterday he caught sight of the bird looking at him. It gave him a hearty laugh and then took off across the yard, flying like some brightly painted World War I biplane, over the fence into the junkyard, dipping around the roof of the old city bus.

Jerry looked for that red head. All he saw was tree. He scratched the back of his bare leg and decided it was too cold to be outside trying to find a bird. Miles away, above the jumbled piles of broken cars and refrigerators and everything else turning to ground, the snowcapped mountain glowed. Another day began with a woodpecker alarm clock.

An hour passed. Cupped in his trailer, Jerry moved about blurring the window as he passed, getting dressed, making coffee and toast. A transistor radio muttered the news of the day.

When he opened the door again, his face was painted, he wore a baggy suit and he held a garbage bag. He was a clown taking out the trash. He dumped it in the bin next to the steps and went back in the trailer. Other birds were awake and singing. Some of them transmitted from the acres of metal scrap, distantly, like rusted needles on record grooves.

The next time Jerry appeared, he was wearing a hat. He carried a flat cardboard box to the car in the driveway. Daisies grew in patches in the grass around the tires. After a long wet winter and a lot of rainy April days, the muddy yard was deep green.

Paying no attention to birds or flowers, Jerry put the box on the backseat, got behind the wheel and started the ignition. The engine turned over clumsily, gnashing and coughing out a rusty cloud. He knew it was living on borrowed time. Anytime it really needed help, he fished for parts in the junkyard next door. A slat in the fence could swing aside to let him through. Sooner or later, there would be nothing more he could do and the old red car with Jerry the Clown painted in yellow would make that last ride to the other side. He knew a guy over there; maybe he would give him something in trade.

The library was only five minutes away. Jerry could have taken his bicycle, but he had an important errand to run in his little car that could fit ten clowns.

A street lined with trees became a town and he turned into a parking lot. There were plenty of spots to leave his car. He reached over the seat, grabbed his box and got out.

The early morning air was cool as water. The trees along the lot were pink and white and he took a deep breath of cherry. Shaking himself like a wet golden retriever, he trotted in place for a moment. As they liked to say in the spotlight, it was showtime.

The library got bigger with every flapping step he took. Fallen blossoms stuck to his yellow shoes.

The place was full of books, waiting for him and he imagined the authors all noticed him when he opened the door. The shelves rattled just the smallest bit.

The woman at the counter gave him quite a look. Jerry decided she would be a good start. Her eyes stayed on him as she set down a book.

"Good morning," she smiled. "Can I help you?"

Jerry set his box on the counter between them and opened the flaps. He turned it around so she could read the title on the pile of typed paper. *My Life As A Clown.*

She said, "Oh! Did you write this?"

Jerry nodded. It was his book. This was a library and it only made sense to him that he should bring it here.

"My goodness," she said. "What an achievement."

While she thumbed through the manuscript, Jerry reached behind the cloth flower on his suit and found his notebook and pen. Flipping to a blank page, he quickly wrote a message. He held the page for her to read. He watched her eyes.

She said, "Oh, I'm sure the library would like to add this to our collection, but first it needs to be published. Do you have any experience with that?"

Jerry shook his head. He began to rock back and forth on his long shoes. He couldn't help it, he was nervous.

"Let me get something from our reference section." She turned to the shelving on the wall behind her. She pulled out a book thick as a log of wood. It landed with a thump on the counter next to his manuscript. "Now, this is a listing of all the agents. You just find one that looks like a match for your work then you mail it to them."

Jerry's chin dropped to his shirt.

She laughed, "I know you can do it! Here," she pushed the book towards him, "you take this over to that desk and see what you can find."

He tried. He sat at the table and turned pages but it was like trying to read a telephone book. The Tokyo phone book. He could have spent years wandering the alleyways and looking in windows, knocking on papered walls.

He shut the book. He didn't know anything about Tokyo and all those authors watched him go. The big glass door kept them inside and the moment Jerry pushed it open he heard the birds, still singing away. A loud pickup truck passed in the street adding another layer to the song of the day.

On the parking lot, Jerry slowed to think about that woodpecker at home. He wondered if he should go back in the library to see if there was some book with advice on how to get rid of them. Could you hang things from branches, paint startling images, or set out decoys of their natural enemies?

He supposed there were things you could do, but ultimately you just had to wait it out. Anything with wings wouldn't be around forever; it would get tired of his yard and move on. Yesterday, someone at the café told him it was good luck to have a woodpecker knock on your house. Was it true?

Like canoes, his shoes stopped beside his red clown car. The windshield was covered in cherry blossoms. His hand, fit in an old gray glove, swept the glass clean in one, two, three wet strokes.

# THE BALLAD OF NATURAL SELECTION

Thank you for giving us the opportunity to consider "The Mouth of McKenzie." We regret that the piece does not meet our needs at this time, but we appreciate everyone who shared their work with us.

Thank you very much for letting us see "The Weight of One Moth." We appreciate your taking the time to send it in for our consideration. Although it does not suit the needs of the magazine at this time, we wish you luck with placing it elsewhere.

Thank you for giving me a chance to read "The Weight of One Moth." Unfortunately, this story didn't quite win me over and I'm going to pass on it. I wish you best of luck finding the right market for it and hope that you'll keep us in mind in the future.

At present, your manuscript does not suit our needs. Thank you for giving us the opportunity to consider your work.

## ALMOST ANIMALS

Fes Smurlo and Milo T. Smiley. Nobody had heard of them for years, they had gone off the marquee and fallen off the edge of the world...or so it seemed.

One afternoon, Fes shuffled through a handful of junk mail and stopped on a handwritten envelope. The writing looked like a child's; the peculiar loping letters were almost drawings of animals. Fes tossed the other ads and flyers into the pail next to the wall and studied the fascinating envelope. It had been a long time since he and his partner had received any fan mail.

From behind him, the door opened and an elderly woman crept into the lobby. She wore a bright red windbreaker, sunglasses, and carried a bag in one hand and a long stick in the other. The stick had a claw on the end. She used it to pick up garbage on her walk around the neighborhood and the bag she held was full.

"Hello, Mrs. McCartney," Fes said. She was older than him by a few years. He still thought of her when she owned that house on the corner with the perfect garden and the lawn nobody dared walk across.

"Good afternoon," she replied. She had a heron way of walking, picking each step across the tiled, checkered lily pad floor.

Fes turned and waved the envelope casually, "Looks like I got an actual letter for a change." He chuckled but it sounded dry and phony. There was no getting around it—he was intimidated by those thick dark glasses and that stick with the claw.

She clucked and placed the bag into the garbage can by Fes. They were done talking; she had places to be.

"Have a good evening," Fes said anyway. She was on her way to the elevator and he looked at the envelope again. Had some kid seen Milo and him on a TV rerun? It was possible. Every once in a while they would play their appearance on the old *Sylvan Moore Show*.

On the other side of the letter was a bright yellow sun sticker. It had a smiling face. Fes imagined the kid again, dropping the letter in a blue metal box on the street, saying goodbye and running down the sidewalk. Obviously, this was a magical letter and Fes carried it up the three flights of stairs unopened so he could share it with Milo.

Milo wasn't aware of anything. Blackness surrounded him. He had been in a trance for the longest time. He didn't stir in the darkness as Fes returned and called out his name.

"Milo!" Fes shut the apartment door, "Milo, we got a letter." He laughed, "They still remember us, partner." Over by the bookshelf, Fes reached for a violin case on the floor. "You awake, Milo?" He set the case on the tabletop and flicked the latches and opened the lid.

Milo looked asleep, eyes shut, arms and legs folded over neatly, tucked tight in his vampire's coffin.

Fes left him like that, with the lid open, while he went to the kitchen. There was the sound of a drawer opening, a clatter of silverware, and when Fes found a knife, he tore the envelope along its seam. He stood in the kitchen by the sink in the window light and read it aloud, "Dear Mr. Smurlo and Milo, I hope you are doing very well. My name is Norman Spinnaker and I have a monthly variety show at a local café. It would be an honor to have you two perform for our audience." Fes finished the rest of the note quietly. "What do you think, Milo?"

The doll-sized figure in the other room didn't answer.

"Should we dust off the old act?" Footsteps led Fes back to the table. "What do you say, partner?" It had been so long since he heard the voice of Milo T. Smiley he had to think about it for a minute. It came from the back of the throat, an irritating rasp pooled like the glossy top layer in an old can of house paint.

By that evening though, Milo was chattering away, even as Fes put him back into the violin case and carried him along the sidewalk, locked up tight.

Fes only stopped once in his walk. The weather had been sunny since afternoon, not a cloud in the sky, the first swallows of the season flying over the abandoned lot. Three blocks from the café, Fes had to stop to watch a raccoon that was halfway up a tree, looking out a window in the trunk. It was hypnotized by the sunset.

The violin case gave a twitch as Milo kicked it a couple times.

"Okay, Milo. Sorry, I was watching something." When he started to walk, the raccoon didn't notice him leave. Milo calmed down. Fes thought about it and wondered if he could work that into their act.

They turned onto a busier street where spindly trees were planted in the cement like brooms and cars followed each other. On the other side was a laundromat, a boarded up store, and a crowd around the café on the corner. "There it is, Milo. Le Beatnik café. Looks like quite a crowd is here to see us."

As Fes and Milo jaywalked across the street, a great cheer went up from all the long shadows on the corner. Mid-smile, Fes was about to describe their welcome, when he realized it was for a pack of dogs passing through the open door. The dogs were followed by a couple dressed in sequin tuxedos, clucking out orders. Everyone's cheers reminded Fes of their own glory days. Once, they were described as the next Bergen & McCarthy. And then Milo decided to go solo. He got on a train for

Wichita and sent Fes a postcard when he got there alone. Those were rough times while they were apart. When Milo returned, they were quiet about that time.

Slipping in with the crowd, nobody seemed to recognize Fes with his shabby suit and violin case. He passed the words Le Beatnik painted on the bay window. Inside, lanterns were strung along the ceiling, a good turnout; it looked like standing room only. Fes wanted to think their act had something to do with that. A bright poster was taped on the glass door: *Tonight! Alexander's Dogtime Band. Fes Smurlo & Milo T. Smiley. Johnson Dracula.*

Fes didn't like to follow an animal act. He supposed people said the same thing about ventriloquists. Then he wondered what Johnson Dracula planned on doing—was he going to turn into a bat?

After being pushed along, Fes stopped beside the wall, with a pretty good view of the stage. The place was buzzing all around him like a candlelit honeycomb. A jazz record was playing. Someone held onto a pillar and beat it like a drum. A dog was barking near the curtains.

Fes was excited to be back in the limelight. He held the violin case up so he could talk to it. "We're here, Milo."

There might have been a muffled reply, but it was hard to tell.

Pressed to the wall, Fes felt like a hat rack in the dark excited room full of dog lovers. People bumped him and laughed and nodded to the music. It's okay, Fes consoled himself, I've been on stages all over the world, on the radio, TV. Reminded that he was a star, he could calm his jittery nerves and the butterflies that banged around beneath his vest.

At last, a shambling man in an overcoat tugboated onto stage, leaning heavily on a cane. He held up a hand and the room quieted. "Good evening," he said, "I'm Norman Spinnaker. Welcome to Le Beatnik." Applause and a dog barked. "I must say you're in luck tonight. Of course you've already noticed some of the talent. We have a dog act that's out of this world. We also have a…" he paused for the clapping to stop, "We have a local man you're bound to find fascinating." He shaded his eyes to search the audience, "Mister Fes Smurlo, are you here yet?"

"Yes!" Fes waved. "Over here!"

"Wonderful! And you brought Milo T. Smiley?"

"Yes, yes." He shook the violin case in the air.

Norman chuckled. "That's our second act, ladies and gentlemen." There was a polite reaction to that announcement. "And finally, once the night has really settled in, we have a favorite of yours waiting in the wings, a hometown hero, the legendary Johnson Dracula." A great cheer erupted and the dogs behind the curtain howled in unison. "So without further ado, let's prepare the stage for Alexander's Dogtime Band!"

While everyone clapped, two women, probably waitresses, brought out a miniature drum set and piano. They left them where Norman had been speaking. A spotlight settled on them and the lanterns dimmed.

A dog act is pretty much what you would expect, even one playing New Orleans jazz. Soon, Fes moved along the wall towards the door. The cooler night air slipped in from the street.

Like someone in a rowboat trailing a lively steam liner, Fes stood curbside, staring at the light in the café window. The muffled sound of barking harmony and steady applause roared like a seashell held to the ear. It would be a hard act to follow.

The violin case rocked in his hand and Fes remembered Milo. "Okay," he said. It was too bad there wasn't a dressing room; all they had was the street. Some few steps away, in front of the shuddered storefront, Fes set the case flat on top of a car hood and unlatched the lid.

Milo sat up and took a deep breath. His monocle flashed and he held out his thin arms and cried, "O Captain! my Captain! our fearful trip is done, the ship has weather'd every rack, the prize we sought is won!"

"Oh no!" Fes clapped a hand over the dummy's wooden mouth. This was what he feared, even after all that time locked in a violin case. "You can't do that material! Don't you remember what happened when you went on the road with that?" He gave Milo a shake.

"Don't you remember Kansas? They ate you alive! Listen to me." Fes removed his hand, "We have to stick together. No more poetry, we have to stick to our routine." He let go of Milo. "Okay, let's just try one joke to get in the zone." He faced the car and said, "Thank you, thank you, what a great audience. I'm reminded of when I went to meet Milo's folks. They were pine trees!"

Milo slapped his forehead.

Fes continued, "Say, how's that—"

"I can't do this," Milo groaned.

"What?"

Milo put a hand on his heart to emote, "You taught me language…The red plague rid you for leaving me your language!"

"Oh no," said Fes. "Not this again."

Milo leaped off the hood, into the open window of a passing car and was gone just like that. So much for their big break…Fes would have to tell Norman it was all over, and he would have to go home to the apartment alone, to watch for a letter from Kansas.

# THE BARN OWL

The wind swept across the big pond behind the barn. An invisible river blew between the poplars out by the road and waved the tall grass aside like green long bottom weeds.

When it hit the barn, warped and worn by the rain, crooked boards made silver as fish skin, there was a music in the creaks and ticks. The steady hiccup of a rope that hung from a rafter.

Up in the broken roof slat, an owl was dreaming his flight above nighttime fields full of mice. He could turn into air silently. But wise as the owl was, he didn't know he slept while the wind blew. He was in a dream apart from everything. He forgot he was also in this world, held together precariously and waiting for that one last breath to fall.

# THE COLD ROOM

It's a family ghost story that's traveled through time and it begins with a room. This was one of those haunted rooms of childhood. It was all wood, painted sea green and nautical cold. It would be roasting hot summer outside, but not in there. It was always winter and it always looked like fresh wet paint on the walls and dresser. The bed was a block pushed in the corner, cold blankets tucked tight. You can imagine, it wasn't often I slept in that sea chest room.

One time we were talking in the kitchen. We liked to have coffee together, and a spark in our conversation got my grandmother up and she went into that room. She came back with something she kept hidden in there. She wanted me to hold the folded 40-year-old paper from the Navy. A telegram about her brother.

My uncle wrote me last year and told me how it happened.

*Jimmy was killed by a kamikaze strike while off*

*Okinawa on 28 May 1945. I remember the day that the two Navy officers came to the house with the news of Jimmy's loss and talked with Mom. I was 6 at the time and remember it like it happened yesterday. Jimmy was a Fireman First Class aboard USS Drexler, at that time on radar picket duty in support of the invasion of Okinawa—we lost a lot of ships and sailors to kamikaze attacks during that period. Drexler was hit by two kamikaze aircraft and went down in less than a minute.*

When I finished reading, she folded him again and put him back in that room. I heard the drawer of the dresser open and close.

I've done a lot of thinking about this. Even though it happened a long time ago and people have come and gone, I see it happening like a movie.

At 5 AM on a spring morning, nine warplanes left Japan and flew over the ocean. After two hours of blue, the air was full of tracer bullets and flak. There were eleven fliers, aged 18-21. They were led by a 29-year-old commander whose wife and children had drowned themselves in the Arakawa River that winter. By then pilots were getting scarce. You had to be able to hold steady, fly low, ten to twenty feet above the water, and crash.

I also see what happened before. What was it like to wake up that morning, on the ocean? I don't know if Jimmy had time for coffee but I hope so. Radar warned them planes were on the way, alarms and horns and battle stations. Could he feel that rushing cold? Jimmy was 26.

It wasn't over though. He had a wife and two sons and a sister halfway around the world. When two men in uniform came to my grandmother's door, she told them, "I already know." All that was left of him she kept folded in a drawer.

# THE MAN IN THE ATTIC

Some children's show ends with the usual loud music and credits, vanishes for a moment into black and then, as if a lightbulb string has been pulled, the TV screen fills with a new sight. A man is sitting in the attic. It's hard to describe him now, he seems ordinary like someone you'd see buying groceries, and he is calm, talking directly to the camera. After all this time, it's impossible to remember what he said, what his show was about, or why he was stuck in that attic.

# ALMOST ANIMALS
by Allen Frost
All stories (except one) written in Spring 2018

# Books by Good Deed Rain

*Saint Lemonade*, Allen Frost, 2014. Two novels illustrated by the author in the manner of the old Big Little Books.

*Playground*, Allen Frost, 2014. Poems collected from seven years of chapbooks.

*Roosevelt*, Allen Frost, 2015. A Pacific Northwest novel set in July, 1942, when a boy and a girl search for a missing elephant. Illustrated throughout by Fred Sodt.

*5 Novels*, Allen Frost, 2015. Novels written over five years, featuring circus giants, clockwork animals, detectives and time travelers.

*The Sylvan Moore Show*, Allen Frost, 2015. A short story omnibus of 193 stories written over 30 years.

*Town in a Cloud*, Allen Frost, 2015. A three-part book of poetry, written during the Bellingham rainy seasons of fall, winter, and spring.


*A Flutter of Birds Passing Through Heaven: A Tribute to Robert Sund.* 2016. Edited by Allen Frost and Paul Piper. The story of a legendary Ish River poet & artist.


*At the Edge of America*, Allen Frost, 2016. Two novels in one book blend time travel in a mythical poetic America.


*Lake Erie Submarine*, Allen Frost, 2016. A two week vacation in Ohio inspired these poems, illustrated by the author.


*and Light*, Paul Piper, 2016. Poetry written over three years. Illustrated with watercolors by Penny Piper.

*The Book of Ticks*, Allen Frost, 2017. A giant collection of 8 mysterious adventures featuring Phil Ticks. Illustrated throughout by Aaron Gunderson.

*I Can Only Imagine*, Allen Frost, 2017. Five adventures of love and heartbreak dreamed in an imaginary world. Cover & color illustrations by Annabelle Barrett.

*The Orphanage of Abandoned Teenagers*, Allen Frost, 2017. A fictional guide for teens and their parents. Illustrated by the author.

*In the Valley of Mystic Light: An Oral History of the Skagit Valley Arts Scene*, 2017. Edited by Claire Swedberg & Rita Hupy.

*Different Planet*, Allen Frost, 2017. Four science fiction adventures: reincarnation, robots, talking animals, outer space and clones. Cover & illustrations by Laura Vasyutynska.

*Go with the Flow: A Tribute to Clyde Sanborn*. 2018. Edited by Allen Frost. The life and art of a timeless river poet.

*Homeless Sutra*, Allen Frost, 2018. Four stories: Sylvan Moore, a flying monk, a water salesman, and a guardian rabbit.

*The Lake Walker*, Allen Frost 2018. A little novel set in black and white like one of those old European movies about death and life.

*A Hundred Dreams Ago*, Allen Frost, 2018. A winter book of poetry and prose. Cover and illustrations by Aaron Gunderson.

*Almost Animals*, Allen Frost, 2018. A collection of linked stories, thinking about what makes us animals.

www.ingramcontent.com/pod-product-compliance
Lightning Source LLC
LaVergne TN
LVHW041647060526
838200LV00040B/1754